This book belongs to

_____

_____

The
Enchanted
Treasure
AND OTHER MAGICAL STORIES

The
Enchanted
Treasure

AND OTHER MAGICAL STORIES

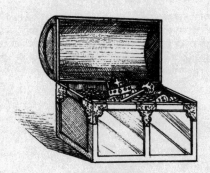

First published in Great Britain in 1998 by
Parragon
13 Whiteladies Road
Clifton
Bristol BS8 1PB

Copyright © Parragon 1998

ISBN 0 75252-527-1

Printed in Great Britain

Produced by Nicola Baxter
PO Box 71
Diss Norfolk IP22 2DT

Stories by Nicola Baxter
Designed by Amanda Hawkes
Text illustrations by Duncan Gutteridge
Cover illustration by Alisa Tingley

Contents

The Enchanted Treasure   9

The Lost Book   33

The Flying Carpet   51

The Friendly Dragon   69

The Conjuror's Secret   89

The Christmas Pudding Wish   121

The Magic Trumpet   133

Aunt Bella's Umbrella   143

The Contrary Princess   155

Wise Wishes   167

The Apple Spell   175

The Elf Who Couldn't Spell   185

The
Enchanted
Treasure

Many people dream of riches and the power that wealth will bring them. They are sure that all the happiness in the world can be theirs for the price of a gold coin or two. A few have been fortunate enough to find the treasure they seek. Others have been luckier still and have not found it. This is the story of a treasure that passed through many hands before it was lost – perhaps for ever.

A long time ago, a King lived in a castle on a hill. He was interested in only one thing – money. He had a beautiful and loving wife and a little daughter

who was a pretty and clever as any little girl in the kingdom, but he could not feel happy until his coffers were full of gold coins and his treasury was piled high with silver plate.

"Tomorrow," he said to himself, "I will play with my daughter and take a stroll in the garden with my wife, but today I must make sure that the money due in rent from my tenants is properly collected. It is true that I am richer than anyone else I know, but hard times may come, and I must be prepared."

Of course, hard times never came. Tomorrow, which he

would spend with his family, never came either. Day after day, the King worked and schemed to increase his wealth.

One day in early spring, a servant came to the King with a pale and tear-stained face.

"I regret to tell you, Your Highness," he said, "that the Queen, your wife, is gravely ill. She is begging to see you."

The King was stunned. Why, he had seen his wife only yesterday … no, last week … no, a few weeks ago perhaps. All of a sudden, the great love he had for her welled up in his heart, and he rushed to where she lay.

As soon as he saw her lying so still and pale on her bed, the King knew that his wife could not live for long. Clasping her hands in his, he cried out loud, so that his voice could be heard all over the castle.

"Oh, I will give every penny I have," he wailed, "to the person who can give my wife back to me. What is money worth without loved ones to share it with?"

How often we understand what we really care for just as we are about to lose it! Yet the King's offer did not go unanswered. As if from nowhere, a little figure appeared at his elbow. It was a goblin wizard, who had been waiting for just this chance.

"Your Highness," he whispered, "I can save your wife if you will give me the gold you promised."

"Yes, yes," cried the King. "Do what you have to do. Everything I have is yours."

The goblin wizard bent over the bed and spoke softly in the pale woman's ear. "It is as I promised," he said. "All that you wished for is here in this room. Live now and be happy."

The Queen stirred and opened her eyes. Beside the bed, her husband's own eyes filled with tears of happiness. Clasping his wife and daughter to him, he said with great emotion, "I have been a foolish man. We shall be poor for ever now in the things of this world, but we shall be richer in the only things that really matter. I thought that money was all that was of value in the world. Now I realise that time is much more precious – time to enjoy what we have been given, before it is too late."

And so the King and his family pass out of our story, for it is the treasure and its fate that we are following.

The goblin wizard had the golden coins and the silver plate

loaded into chests and placed in seven strong carriages. He knew that he could have taken possession of the castle, too, if he had wished, but he had no interest in anything but real treasure. With a small army of hand-picked soldiers to guard the carriages, he set off for his own country.

As the carriages rumbled along, the goblin wizard imagined how he would be greeted. Goblins love gold and riches. Surely his countrymen, who had once driven him from their land because of his idle, cunning ways, would welcome him as a long lost brother! More than anything else, the goblin longed to be praised and admired by his own people. He felt that he had been an outcast all his life. Now it was time for his reward.

But as he travelled, the goblin began to see visions of other futures opening before him. As fond as they were of treasure, might his fellow goblins not steal his golden coins from him, laughing at him as they did so? His army, he knew, would flee in the face of the goblin magic they did not understand. He would be alone and defenceless. And what, in those circumstances, would his life be worth? What goblin, dazzled by the treasure in those chests, would hesitate to kill him for such riches?

At that moment, the goblin wizard realised for the first time that he valued his own life much more highly than all the gold he had won.

"It's not worth the risk," he said to himself. "I shall get rid of this treasure as soon as possible. Then I can live safely and without fear. I have not slept for days, knowing that one of my soldiers might try to steal from me. When the treasure has gone, I shall have a night's peace at last."

But losing a very great treasure is not so easy when you want to do it. As many people have found, it is quite easy to lose something you really want to keep, but very difficult to lose the same thing on purpose. First of all, the goblin began giving gold coins to the poor people he

met on the road, but he found
that they began to follow him,
instead of going back to their
homes and improving their lives
as he had hoped. That was no
good at all. In the end, the goblin
had to ask his soldiers to
frighten the people away.

Next, the goblin thought of burying the treasure. Each night, when the soldiers slept, he would take a little spade and bury as many coins as he could beside the road. Some of the little piles of treasure that the goblin buried are still being found to this day.

But the goblin soon realised that it would take years to get rid of all his treasure in this way. He would have to think of something else.

Just as the goblin was becoming ill with worry, and was feeling as though the whole weight of the treasure was on his

shoulders, the problem was
taken out of his hands.

A gang of robbers was lurking
in a nearby wood. When they
saw the carriages creaking past,
guarded by soldiers, they knew
they must contain something very
valuable. The next night, under
cover of darkness, they attacked!

The battle was short and bitter. Before long, all the soldiers lay wounded and beaten by the side of the road. It was a wonder that none of them was killed. The goblin himself had used what little magic he could remember to escape to a nearby mountain top, where he lived to the end of his days, free at last from the burden of wanting what he did not dare to keep.

Meanwhile, the robbers made off with the seven carriages, taking them deep into the forest along tracks that no one else knew. When they reached their camp, many miles away, they forced open the carriages and looked into the chests inside.

Then, for the first time, they realised what a great treasure they had found, and almost immediately, disputes arose between the robbers.

"Five of the seven carriages belong to me!" shouted the robber chief. "I am your leader, and as such I take the greatest share."

"Not so great a share as that!" cried the other robbers. "We shared in the danger. We should share in the treasure, too."

Before long, the arguments grew hot and fierce. Arguments turned to blows. Blows turned to cudgels and swords. By daybreak, not a single robber was left alive in the forest glade.

Year after year, the treasure lay in open chests under the mighty trees. The bodies of the robbers were covered with leaves and gradually sank into the soil, until not even their bones could be seen. But the golden coins remained untarnished, gleaming in the sunlight and the moonlight as night followed day over and over again.

It was a hundred years later that the treasure was found again. The King of the country decided to wage war on his neighbour, who had fairer lands than his own. He knew that the most important battles would be won or lost at sea, so he was determined to build the greatest navy the world had ever seen. He decreed that the great royal forest should be cut down to supply wood for his ships.

Day after day, the woodcutters worked, felling the mighty oaks that had stood for generations. At last they came to the clearing where the treasure lay.

The woodcutters were honest men. They reported their discovery to the King. Needless to say, the King was delighted. As the treasure was found in a royal forest, he declared that it was definitely royal treasure. He ordered his men to load it on to carts and bring it to the great port nearby, where the King had set up his campaign headquarters.

For many months, the worthy woodcutters continued their work. Then the shipwrights took over. Day after day and night after night, the sound of their saws and hammers and chisels could be heard for miles around.

At last the great fleet sat proudly in the water, its pennants flying. The navy was ready to sail.

As the King prepared to go on board, he realised that he had a problem. He dared not leave his great treasure behind, for he feared that it would be stolen in his absence. After all, he would be taking his army with him. There would be no one left behind to guard the treasure.

"There is only one thing to be done," said the King. "I shall have to take the treasure with me." He ordered his men to load it all on to the greatest ship in the fleet. Then he went on board himself and gave the order to set sail. With a fair wind, the fleet left the harbour.

At first all went well as the mighty galleons sailed across the calm sea, but then a great wind blew up, whipping the waves into peaks higher than the tallest mast. Most of the fleet was blown back to the harbour, where the sailors and soldiers scrambled ashore. But the flagship of the fleet lay heavy in the water with the weight of the treasure on board. She soon began to sink lower and lower, as seawater flooded her decks and holds. The waves towered above her.

The King, clinging to the mast, cried out as another had done before him. "I will give all my treasure, if only I can be saved from this terrible fate! Why, oh why, did I decide to wage war when I could have stayed safely at home?" This time, no passing goblin arrived to save the day. The ship went down, and the King went with it. The caskets of treasure spilled out on to the sandy sea bed.

And that is where they lie now, their contents glittering in the green water. Would it have made a difference to any of the people who came into contact with the treasure if they had known that it was enchanted? Long, long ago, a curse had been put upon the gold and silver.

> *You shall not*
>   *Give lasting pleasure,*
> *But teach what is*
>   *A life's true measure.*

Which of those who saw the glitter of the gold could have walked away from its glow? Would you?

The Lost
Book

I don't suppose there is anyone who has not, at some time or another, lost something they value. It is always distressing, whether it is a single sock or a diamond ring. Sometimes the loss is of something that simply cannot be replaced. That is what happened to Wizard Midnight.

Now Wizard Midnight was not a careless man. He could hardly have been a wizard if he were, for using spells is very detailed work. One slip in the recipe of a spell – a hair from the back of a polar bear instead of a grizzly bear, for example – and disaster can be the result. Many an apprentice wizard has simply disappeared because he did not pay careful attention to the instructions in his *Great Book of Wizardry*.

No, Wizard Midnight was always careful, and he took his work very seriously. He was not one of these up-and-coming wizards who are more interested in clouds of yellow and red smoke than in real magic. But Midnight had been a wizard for a very long time, and that meant that his spellatory (like a laboratory, but for spells) was packed from floor to ceiling with boxes and caskets and jars and – most of all – books.

The names of the books would give you some idea of the many areas of magic that Wizard Midnight had studied. *Princes into Frogs: an illustrated guide* rubbed shoulders with *Verses and Curses: favourite rhymes from the Great Wizards*. At the bottom of a dusty pile near the door, you might find *A Spell Too Far: an unauthorised biography of Wizard Twilight (disappeared)*. Propping up the broken leg of the wizard's chair you might see *Invisibility: a guide for larger wizards*.

Yes, Wizard Midnight was certainly a very well-read wizard, but what he really needed was a secretary or a librarian to help him keep his books in order. There had been a young elf who had helped him once, but really he had been more trouble than he was worth. Several spells had gone seriously wrong because of mistakes he had made. After that, Wizard Midnight decided to work alone.

It was late one night when the wizard made his first Really Big Mistake. The spellatory was lit only by a flickering candle. Wizard Midnight was tired, but he did just want to finish the spell he was working on before he went to bed. He knew that if he did not, he would toss and turn all night with the spell on his mind.

The spell he was working on was quite a small one, but it would be very, very useful to mothers everywhere, so the wizard was keen to complete it as soon as possible. It was a spell for making babies love all the foods that are really good for them, such as vegetables. At last the wizard felt that the spell was right. It would have to be tested, of course, before it could be used on real babies, but he was pretty sure that there would be no unpleasant side effects.

Before he went to bed, the wizard wrote the new spell in the most important book in his library. It was his own special spell book, so important that it didn't even have a name on the cover. It was the book that contained all the spells the wizard found essential every day. Wizard Midnight wrote down the new spell. He signed it with his name and the date, as all wizards are encouraged to do when they first begin to make spells. Then he put down the book and went to bed.

How easy it is to write that! "He put down the book" we say, and it sounds so simple. It *was* so simple. What was not simple was finding the book again next morning, as you will see.

Wizard Midnight rose next morning bright and early. As usual, he decided to begin the day with a little light breakfast of acorn cereal and daisy juice. He didn't go out and pick what he needed for his breakfast. Of course not! He was a wizard! All that was needed was a quick spell over his bowl and cup. But the spell was in the special spell book, and the special spell book was... It began to seem as if things would not be easy.

Yes, where was that book? The wizard remembered as clearly as anything putting it down the night before. It must be somewhere near his chair. But which of the chairs in the spellatory had he been sitting on last night? It was really rather difficult to remember.

Never mind. The wizard knew a simple little spell for finding any book in his library. He had spent three or four weeks inventing it after the impossible elf had been sent on his way. At least, when I say that the wizard "knew" the spell, I mean that he had it written down, so that he could use it at a moment's notice. And where was it written? Oh dear…

"I am a wizard," said Midnight to himself. "I can and I will find a way out of this mess. But first I really must have some breakfast."

There was nothing for it. Midnight had to go outside and gather some toadstools with his own hands. His special spell for making sure they were not poisonous was in his special spell book, so he had to think carefully about it and then just hope for the best. (Don't try this yourselves unless you know the antidote spell, as Wizard Midnight did.)

Getting breakfast without magic took much more time than usual. Wizard Midnight found that half the morning had disappeared before he was able to start looking for his spell book. Now where was that book?

All day the wizard searched. He stared at the titles of his

books until they began to dance in front of his eyes. Surely he had just seen *Wizardry for Beginners* in another pile? He must be getting confused. (In fact, the wizard was not getting confused at all. He had two copies of *Wizardry for Beginners* because both his grandmothers had given him the book when he first went to wizard school.)

That night, Wizard Midnight went to bed with a heavy heart. Where could that book be?

It was beginning to cross his mind for the first time that something more than simple carelessness might have happened to the book.

What, for example, if another wizard had crept in while Wizard Midnight slept and spirited the book away? What if a magic spell, cast hundreds of miles away, had misfired and made his book invisible? What if a jealous witch, eager to get her own back for being beaten in last year's Master Magician Contest, had sent her black cat to "borrow" the book? The more Wizard Midnight thought about it, the more sure he was that there had been some malicious magic done.

What could he do about it? It is almost impossible to reverse a spell if you do not know what the first spell was. It is definitely impossible if you do not even know for sure that a spell has been used in the first place.

Wizard Midnight thought and thought. He couldn't sleep and he couldn't eat. Only one thing ran through his mind. At all costs, he must get that book back. Not only was his life's work between those covers, but he dreaded to think what would happen if the book fell into the wrong hands.

It took Wizard Midnight two weeks of concentrated thinking and worrying to come up with an idea. He couldn't undo whatever spell had been put on him or his book, but he could go back in time to the last moment he had held the book in his hands. It would be a difficult spell – time travelling is one of the hardest branches of magic – but not impossible. Wizard Midnight decided to start work right away.

The spell took much longer to develop than was usually the case. The wizard's special spell book had contained many useful hints and tips, as well as a number of important short cuts. This time, Wizard Midnight had to manage without any of them.

It was spring when Wizard Midnight lost his book, but it was autumn when he finally finished his time-reversing spell. Brown leaves were beginning to rustle under his door as he prepared to try his spell.

Obviously, I cannot tell you the whole spell, but some of it went like this:

The pages of the book of time
Turn as each night follows day,
Turn them back again in rhyme
And past and present fade away.

Trembling with excitement, the wizard recited the whole spell. There was a shimmering strangeness in the spellatory, and he suddenly found himself sitting late at night, his special spell book in his hands and a daffodil in a vase on his desk.

What did the wizard do next? He looked down at his newly written baby-food spell. He was very tired. He put down his book...

What more can I tell you of Wizard Midnight? In his spellatory, spring becomes summer, and summer becomes autumn. And autumn becomes spring. Winter – and the future – never come.

The
Flying
Carpet

What do you give a wizard who has everything for his birthday? Any wizard worth his salt can magic whatever he needs at any time of day or night. It is pointless giving him socks or boxes of chocolates or aftershave. (Most wizards grow beards in any case, so there isn't any *shave* to come *after*.)

The only thing you can really give a wizard is something new in the magic line – a book of spells, perhaps, or a special magic stirring stick. That is why a little elf called Esmerelda went into Mrs Magglepaggle's Magic Shop one Saturday morning.

"I'm looking for a birthday present for my uncle," she explained. "He's a wizard, and it's so hard to find him anything he couldn't magic up for himself."

"My dear, I know just what you mean," replied Mrs Magglepaggle, who was such a good saleswoman she could have sold ears to elves. "I have just the same trouble," she went on, "with my old grandfather. Have you considered something in the clothing line? Many wizards are wearing old-fashioned robes that do nothing for their figures. What about a new elasticated wizard suit?"

She showed Esmerelda a rather garish creation in shiny green stretchy stuff, with a pattern of stars around the hem.

"I don't quite see Uncle Albertus in that," said the little elf. "I was thinking more of something to help him with his magic."

"Seven-league boots?" suggested Mrs Magglepaggle. "They're coming back into fashion in a big

way, even if we don't have leagues
any more. Or what about a nice
new wand? These ones are made
of aluminium – so much lighter
to carry."

"No, no," cried Esmerelda. She
was beginning to think that it
had been a mistake to come into
the shop. She looked around at
the shelves and noticed what
looked like a rolled-up rug in a
corner at the back.

"What is that, please?" she
asked politely.

Mrs Magglepaggle rolled out
the carpet with one swift
movement. It looked as though a
mouse had been nibbling one

corner, and the colours were rather faded.

"As you can see," said the saleswoman, "it has seen better days, which is why I could let you have it at a very reasonable price. Normally, a carpet like this would cost you a king's ransom. At one time, it was a magic carpet, capable of flying all over the world, but it has lost almost all its magic. The best it can manage now is a little hover around the level of your knees. It gets exhausted after five minutes and flops down again."

"I see," said Esmerelda slowly. In truth, she felt rather sorry for the carpet, and she liked the pattern. "I'll take it," she said firmly, "but I shall want a large discount for wear and tear."

Mrs Magglepaggle did drop the price a good deal. She felt that the carpet made her shop look rather shabby, and although she had sold quite a lot of secondhand magic items at one time, she had decided recently to concentrate on new things. There was more demand for them.

Esmerelda took the carpet home and wrapped it up in lots and lots of silver paper. Then she carried it carefully to her uncle's woodland house.

"Happy Birthday, Uncle Albertus!" she called, as she pushed open the front door.

Uncle Albertus was relaxing in his favourite chair. He was not a very energetic wizard. He felt that he deserved a rest on his birthday. However, he jumped to his feet when he saw his little niece and the bulky parcel she was carrying.

"My dear, you shouldn't have!" he cried, running to help her. "I hope you haven't spent too much of your pocket money on your old uncle."

"No, I haven't," said Esmerelda, perhaps with more truth than politeness. "It didn't cost very much because it's old."

Uncle Albertus was busy undoing the paper. As he rolled out the carpet he gave a little gasp. "My dear, do you know what we have here? It's a genuine, first class, original Arabian flying carpet."

"Is that good?" asked Esmerelda, who knew very little about carpets. "I'm afraid it's not much use, as it doesn't fly very much any more."

"Of course it doesn't," replied her uncle, his eyes gleaming. "No carpet can fly in this condition. It needs a good cleaning and a little magic thread to mend these holes. Then, my dear, it will be as good as new and a very special carpet indeed. Come back tomorrow, when I have had a chance to do a little work on it. Then you will see something extraordinary."

Esmerelda did not need much encouragement. She was so very

pleased to have given her uncle
something he really liked. And
she was eager to see the new
carpet in action.

Next morning, she arrived
early at her uncle's house. She
found him with a duster around
his head and a carpet beater in
his hand. He made a rather grand
gesture with the carpet beater in
the direction of his ceiling.
Esmerelda looked up. There was
the carpet, as large as life. It was
floating just below the ceiling, its
colours gleaming and its little
mouse holes now invisible. As
she watched, the little elf saw
the magic carpet shake itself

vigorously, like a puppy coming out of a pond.

"Yes, it's very frisky this morning," said Uncle Albertus. "Would you like to try it? I'll just call it down. Now where's my Arabic phrase book?"

Esmerelda didn't understand what he said next, but it sounded quite impressive. "It's what you use to hail a taxi in Cairo," explained her uncle, "but it seems to work with carpets too. Hop on!"

Esmerelda quite expected the carpet to flop to the floor under the weight of an elf and a rather large uncle, but it felt quite firm and energetic as she sat down, rather like a powerful horse.

"Are you ready?" asked Uncle Albertus. "Hold on tight. It may be quite vigorous to begin with."

With a flip and a flap, the carpet zoomed out of the door and high up into the air.

"Where are we going?" shouted Esmerelda, above the noise of the wind.

"Wherever we like!" called her uncle. "All we have to do is to think of where we want to be!"

Esmerelda at once thought of a rather beautiful beach she had once visited on holiday. At once the carpet began to spin. Round

and round it went, until the little
elf was dizzy and wishing she
could get off.

"Stop thinking!" called her
uncle. "We're both thinking of
different places and the carpet
doesn't know which way to go."

Esmerelda was so dizzy now
that she could hardly think
anyway. At once, the carpet
stopped spinning and set off at a
steady pace in a northerly
direction instead.

"I've always wanted to visit the
North Pole!" called her uncle,
"but you need terribly strong
magic in cold places. I was never
quite able to manage it before."

"But it will be cold!" objected Esmerelda, whose beach had been wonderfully warm and sunny.

"Don't worry," cried her uncle, doing a quick bit of magic. At once, they were both dressed in warm clothes and holding hot water bottles to be on the safe side. "That's the sort of magic I can manage," laughed Uncle Albertus.

The North Pole, when they reached it, was a little bit of a disappointment. There was nothing there but ice and snow in every direction.

"I thought there would be polar bears," said Esmerelda,

"and a sort of signpost, pointing south, you know."

"So did I," said Uncle Albertus. "Ah well, time to go home, my dear, I suppose."

This time, with both of them thinking of the same place, the carpet travelled at double-quick speed. In no time at all, they were back in Uncle Albertus' house.

"Time for a cup of dandelion tea!" cried the wizard, waving his wand. "Will you be mother?"

Esmerelda laughed and picked up the teapot. It was rather unfortunate that just at that moment the carpet decided to give a shimmy and a shake. The

poor little elf dropped the teapot
and hot tea splashed all over the
magic carpet.

If carpets can be said to yelp,
that's exactly what this carpet
did. In less time that it takes to
read this sentence, it had
whisked itself out from under
their feet and hurtled out of the
door. Uncle Albertus fished out
his Arabic phrase book and tried
saying "a thousand, thousand
pardons" and "forgive your
unworthy servant", but the
carpet did not return.

"I'm afraid we've seen the last
of it," said the wizard with a sigh.
"It was bound to happen. Those

thoroughbred carpets are very highly strung. But it was a wonderful present, my dear, and I thoroughly enjoyed my trip to the North Pole, even if there weren't any polar bears."

Apparently, the carpet has been sighted in several parts of the world since that day. If you should happen to hop on it by mistake one day, hold on tight and think hard of where you would like to go. Oh ... and do try not to drop tea on it!

The
Friendly
Dragon

Everyone knows that most dragons are not friendly. They breathe fire for one thing, which is never comfortable for those near them. After all, even if he isn't trying to burn you to a frazzle, a dragon might become absentminded just for a moment and forget not to breathe. It would only take a sort of a snort to turn you into toast.

Because dragons are known to be a problem for ordinary mortals, most people keep well clear of them. It's not hard to find out where they are living, for their caves always look rather burnt around the edges and smell of smoke. People in nearby towns and villages know which hillsides to avoid and always consult their noses about the smokiness of the air before they go along a forest path.

This was all very well in the days when there was a dragon on every mountain. From time to time, dragons would get together and exchange ideas. Then smoke would rise from the mountains as their hot breaths mingled in the air above.

But in recent years, there have been fewer and fewer dragons. Some say that they are related to the ancient dinosaurs, who once roamed our earth. Like them, they will all die out in time.

Others say that all dragons have learned to live underground, where they sometimes make the earth shake. Whatever is happening, there simply are not so many dragons about these days, which is a relief in lots of ways.

It is very rare now for a laundry woman to find that all her washing has been scorched on the line. On the other hand, there are more forest fires than there used to be. Dragons were very good at sniffing a different kind of smoke on the air, and would go and stamp out any smouldering timbers with their big feet. Nowadays, that hardly ever happens, and the fire is fanned until huge trees catch alight.

All of this means that life is much harder for the few remaining dragons than it used to be. People in nearby villages have forgotten how to live with a dragon in their neighbourhood, and dragons have become rather lonely. The chances of getting together with other dragons are very slim now. A dragon might spend hundreds of years on his own, spending his days and nights alone without ever seeing a fire-breathing brother.

That is exactly what happened not so long ago near the village of Frazzle in the Wild Mountains. Those mountains were not so very wild at the time of this story, but they did still have one single dragon living in a cave near the top. Everyone knew he was there, but as they saw no sign of him for year after year, there were always rumours flying about that he had died at last.

Then, of course, a few brave lads would climb up the mountain to check, for everyone knows that each dragon keeps a hoard of gold deep in his cave. To get hold of the gold, you have to wait until the dragon has died, or be prepared to fight him for it. Dragon-fighting is not taught in our military schools today, so it is a long time since a knight tackled a real dragon.

As they climbed, the lads would look out for signs of dragon activity – twigs that were broken or scorched, for example. Always they came back to the village, saying, "We didn't see him, but he's definitely still there."

As time passed, the dragon grew more and more lonely. He used to spend hour after hour happily counting his gold and warming its cold surfaces with the fire from his nostrils. Now, even that activity was beginning to bore him. It seemed so empty somehow.

What this dragon really wanted was a friend – someone he could discuss fire-breathing and compare gold pieces with. But he knew perfectly well that there was not another dragon for miles around. There was only one thing for it. He would have to find a human friend.

The dragon was pretty sure that humans were interested in fire and gold too. He thought he might be able to find someone who would like to come for a chat now and then. In return, he might be able to do something useful for them. He could heat-strip their paintwork perhaps, when they wanted to redecorate, or heat their bath water when there was a power cut.

With this in mind, the dragon set off bright and early one morning for the nearby village.

It was not encouraging that the very first person he came across flew screaming into his house at the first sight of the dragon's green and yellow face.

"Never mind," said the dragon to himself. "There will be some braver people in the village. Not everyone likes dragons. I do understand that. Not all dragons like humans, after all."

But as the dragon approached the village, more and more people ran screaming from him. It was unheard of for a dragon to come into a town or village. They were sure that they were all about to be burnt in their beds.

The dragon hung around in the main square for a while. He even tried peering in a few windows. No one came out at all. After a while, he trotted unhappily back towards the mountain.

As soon as he had gone, there was great activity in the village. A meeting was called in the main square, and everyone got together to decide what must be done.

Desperately, they turned first to old Angus.

"You're the only person still alive who received the old dragon-fighting training," they said. "You must go and fight him, so that he doesn't come back."

"Don't be ridiculous," cried Angus. "I'm eighty-five! I can't go fighting dragons at my age! Besides, he looked like quite a young dragon to me – two or three hundred years old at the most – he could run rings round me any day."

There was some sense in Angus' words, but no one could think of anything else to do. At least, not anything sensible.

"We could build a great big wooden fence around the village," said one bright spark, "so that he couldn't get in."

"And where would be get the wood from?" asked Angus.

"Why, the forest, of course."

"And where is the forest?"

"Don't be silly. It's all over the mountain."

"And who lives at the top of the mountain?"

"Oh…"

Other suggestions were no better. Could they somehow put out the dragon's fire with water from a hose? Could they sneak up one night and put bars across his cave? Could they send someone out to dig a big pit that he could fall into? All these ideas met with the same problem. No one was brave enough to volunteer to go and carry them out.

At last a little voice piped up. It was a little boy who was new to the village. He had come to live with his aunt the year before and knew what it was like to feel an outsider and alone.

"I think," he said, "that I could just talk to the dragon. You know, have a chat and find out why he came down from his cave. Then we'll know what to do."

That sounded a sillier idea than all the others put together, but it was the only idea that had a volunteer attached to it. Before long, the villagers had agreed. Next morning, the little boy would climb up to the dragon's cave at the top of the mountain and have a few words with him.

"We'll never see him again," said Angus, shaking his head. "But if the boy wants to go…" Deep down, everyone wondered if the dragon had been just a tiny bit hungry. They used to eat princesses, didn't they, in the old days? They were pretty sure that the boy was about to become breakfast.

But next morning, the boy found that he would not need to climb the mountain. For the dragon once again came wandering through the village. When he sat down in the middle of the main square, the boy went bravely out to meet him.

"Hello," said the boy, politely.

"Hello," said the dragon. "Er … I'm a dragon."

"I know," said the boy. "I'm called Tom."

"Oh, I'm Sxbvfnxzs," said the friendly dragon.

"I don't think I can pronounce that," said Tom. "May I just call you Dragon?"

"Certainly," said Sxbvfnxzs.

"The thing is," said Tom, "we were wondering why you came to visit us yesterday. And today."

"It's a little hard to explain…" began the dragon, but he did.

For several hours, the dragon and the boy sat in the square and talked. "What's happening out there?" asked the villagers behind their curtains. "Has he eaten him yet?"

But Tom and the dragon were having a perfectly friendly conversation. Towards the end of the afternoon, the dragon gave Tom a jolly smile and ambled off back to his cave.

At once, all the villagers rushed out and surrounded the boy.

"What did he say?"

"What took you so long?"

"Does he speak English?"

"Will he be back?"

Tom held up his hand. "He speaks English," he said, "and, yes, he will be back. He's rather lonely up on his mountain, now that there are no other dragons to visit. He'd like to come down to the village sometimes for a chat. Once a year would be fine, he says, as time goes much more quickly for dragons than it does for us."

The villagers were stunned. A friendly dragon on their doorsteps? Who had ever heard of such a thing? The Mayor's eyes began to gleam. This might be the biggest tourist attraction of all time. Visit Frazzle and Dine with Dragons!

"But he would like his visits to be absolutely secret," Tom went on firmly.

The Mayor's face fell. "Isn't there any room for ... er ... negotiation here?" he asked.

"Well," said Tom, "he could burn down a few of our houses instead if you like."

"No, no, no," said the Mayor. "Absolute secrecy will be fine."

And that is how the matter was left. The dragon was happy. Tom was happy. Even the Mayor was happy. What's that? No, I'm afraid you won't find Frazzle on any map. Absolute secrecy is absolute secrecy after all!

The
Conjuror's
Secret

Mr Wizzy packed his bags carefully. He always made a last-minute check of all his equipment before he went to a performance. It would be a disaster if he cried "Hey presto!" and there were no flowers *up* his sleeve to come bursting *out*! For Mr Wizzy was a conjuror.

Now there are conjurors and conjurors. Some do wonderful tricks and hold you spellbound as they make things appear and disappear. Long strings of coloured flags are pulled out of their mouths. Clouds of blue smoke appear as they finish a trick. Sometimes they even seem to be able to tell what you are thinking, as they guess what is in your pockets or which card you have chosen.

But you know, those tricks are just that – tricks. They are the result of years and years of practice, but if you had the time and wanted to badly enough, you could learn to do most of those tricks yourself.

Some conjurors are different. They do *real* magic. Yes, they really do make things appear and disappear. The things don't just *seem* to be there or not there. They have really appeared out of nothing or actually disappeared into thin air. And if those magicians seem to know what you are thinking, look out!

As you probably know, there are lots and lots of the first kind of conjuror. You may well have been to a party or a show where one has performed. But the *real* magicians are very few and far between. Sometimes you may not even realise that you have met one.

Mr Wizzy was the second kind of conjuror. He had special powers, which he took very seriously. Early on in his career, when he first realised that he really could do magic, Mr Wizzy made a solemn vow. He promised to use his magic only to give people pleasure, never to get things for himself or to harm anyone. And up to the point where this story begins, he had always kept his promise. It was when he broke it – just once – that things began to go wrong.

We left Mr Wizzy carefully packing things for his show that afternoon. He was due to appear in the children's ward of the local hospital. It was almost Christmas, and Mr Wizzy had been booked to give the children a special treat. Most of them would not be able to go home for

Christmas, so the nurses and doctors always tried to make things extra special on the ward.

As Mr Wizzy was getting ready, his doorbell rang.

"Well, dash my buttons," said Mr Wizzy, "who can that be, just as I'm getting ready?"

He hurried to the front door, trying to tie his bow tie with one hand as he went.

Standing on the doorstep was Mr Wizzy's next-door neighbour, Mrs Bizzybee. She was the most talkative woman for miles around, and Mr Wizzy gave a little groan as he saw her standing there.

"Oh, Mr Wizzy," said Mrs Bizzybee, "I-do-hope-you-don't-mind-me-disturbing-you-in-the-middle-of-the-afternoon-like-this-but-my-cat-Whiskers-you-know-the-one-with-a-black-face-and-a-brown-body-and-a-white-tip-to-his-tail-not-the-one-with-the-little-pink-face-and-white-socks-that's-Angelica-not-Whiskers-oh-but-Whiskers-has-gone-missing-and-I-can't-find-him-anywhere-and-I'm-so-very-afraid-he-may-have-gone-on-to-that-busy-main-road-not-the-one-going-to-Elmville-but-the-other-one-you-know-the-one-going-to-Turnytown-and-I-don't-know-what-to-do-can-you-help?"

Phew! That's just how Mrs
Bizzybee talked, without taking a
breath. By the time she had
finished, Mr Wizzy felt exhausted
and he hadn't the faintest idea
what she wanted him to do.

Mrs Bizzybee took a deep
breath. Mr Wizzy could see that
she was just about to begin all
over again. She must be stopped
at all costs! Mr Wizzy began
talking just as fast as she had,
just to keep her quiet.

"Oh, Mrs Bizzybee," he said,
rushing through to his sitting
room and picking up his
conjuring case and the basket
with his animal helpers, "I'm-not-

sure-what-you-want-me-to-do-to-
help-but-I-haven't-got-time-to-
stop-so-I'll-just-er-think-very-
hard-about-it-like-this-*Wizzy-
Kizzy-help-Mrs-Bizzy-give-her-
everything-she-wants!*-and-now-I-
must-go-perhaps-you-can-shut-
the-front-door-for-me-oh-thank-
you-goodbye!"

Double phew! In his hurry to
get out of the house and away
from Mrs Bizzybee, Mr Wizzy
had forgotten his own most
important rule. He had said a
little spell to make everything all
right for his neighbour, but he
hadn't really done it to help her.
He had done it for his own

convenience so that he could get away quickly.

As Mr Wizzy drove away, he didn't even think about what he had done. In fact, he had said the spell so quickly that he hadn't concentrated properly on the words. He hadn't simply asked for Mrs Bizzybee to find her missing cat, he had asked for her to have *everything* she wanted!

It is a pity that Mr Wizzy didn't look in his mirror as he sped down the road. He would have seen Mrs Bizzybee standing on his doorstep in absolute amazement, with Whiskers in her arms, several diamond tiaras on her head and weighing about half as much as she had two minutes before. Things became even more confusing for Mrs Bizzybee when she got home five minutes later to find that each of her three daughters suddenly found herself the proud mother of twins, so that Mrs Bizzybee had all the grandchildren she had ever longed for.

Now you can see as well as I can that this kind of magic is disastrous. What kind of a world would it be if anyone who could do magic just said the first thing that came into his or her head, as Mr Wizzy had just done?

Mr Wizzy, however, was as yet unaware of the havoc he had left behind him. He arrived at the hospital in good time and carried his conjuring case and basket into the children's ward.

The nurses had kindly pulled the curtains across at the end of the ward, so that Mr Wizzy could get all his things ready without the children seeing. Once again, the conjuror checked his equipment. In the back of his mind, he had just the tiniest feeling that something was a little bit wrong, but he couldn't for the life of him think what it was. To tell you the truth, in spite of his many years of experience, Mr Wizzy always got rather nervous before a performance. That is perhaps why he was not thinking straight as he prepared to give his show.

At last it was time for the magic show to begin. Mr Wizzy made a noise like a trumpet fanfare, and the nurses whisked back the curtains. How the children clapped and cheered when they saw Mr Wizzy. They did not know that things were about to go badly wrong.

Mr Wizzy always liked to start his act with a bang – a real bang. As usual, he threw his top hat up into the air, clapped his hands and … the hat dropped to the ground and rolled away under the nearest bed.

Well, of course, that is not at all what was supposed to happen. When Mr Wizzy clapped his hands, he always said a little disappearing spell, and the hat just vanished into thin air. Mr Wizzy was pretty sure that he had got the spell right. He couldn't understand why it didn't work.

The show must go on, and Mr Wizzy was nothing if not professional. With a flourish, he reached into his coat and pulled out … his handkerchief. Oh dear, that was wrong too. It shouldn't have been a handkerchief that appeared but a white dove, which would flutter up to the ceiling and sit quietly nearby until it was time to go home with the conjuror.

Mr Wizzy was becoming quite flustered now. Over the years, he had begun to use more and more real magic in his act, so that he relied on it a good deal. His ordinary conjuring skills were really quite rusty. Mr Wizzy felt a sinking feeling in his tummy. He was pretty sure now that he knew what was happening, and it was

something quite, quite dreadful.
Mr Wizzy had completely lost his
magic powers!

Mr Wizzy looked very red as
he glanced at the children's
expectant faces. He couldn't for
the life of him think what to do.
The full horror of the situation
was just breaking upon him, and
for the first time, he knew *exactly*
why it was happening.

If only he hadn't used that silly
spell on Mrs Bizzybee. He had
broken his promise, and as a
result, his magic had deserted
him. Mr Wizzy thought with
dread of the situation he might
find when he got home. He now

realised how hasty he had been in casting Mrs Bizzybee's spell. He couldn't remember exactly what he had said, but he was pretty sure that the results could spell the end of his life as a conjuror for ever.

Mr Wizzy gazed miserably at his audience. They looked back at him, waiting for a wonderful trick. Then, suddenly, they all began to laugh and clap their hands. Mr Wizzy was confused for a moment, then he looked down and saw with amazement that his white rabbit, Alonso, was doing a tap dance on the table top!

Mr Wizzy was a natural showman, but he was so stunned by the sight of his tap-dancing rabbit that he didn't know what to do. Then the rabbit hissed at him out of the corner of his mouth, "Music! Give me some music!" Almost mechanically, Mr Wizzy began to sing in time with the rabbit's dancing. The children could hardly believe their eyes as the rabbit did a triple somersault with twist as the climax of his dance. Then he bowed several times to his audience, and Mr Wizzy, coming to his senses at last, smiled and bowed too.

"And now," said Mr Wizzy grandly, " Alonso the Magnificent will perform another amazing trick! Take it away, Alonso!"

Alonso extended his right paw. Mr Wizzy hesitated for a moment, then placed his magic wand in the rabbit's grasp. Alonso waved the wand once, twice, three times, and a shower of little stars fell from the ceiling on to the heads of the children watching. It was lovely to see them laugh and stretch up their little hands to try to catch the falling sparklers. But the stars were like bubbles. As soon as they touched something, they vanished.

The rabbit bowed again. Then he waved his wand and pointed to Mr Wizzy's pocket. This time, Mr Wizzy picked up his cue straight away. He felt in his pocket and pulled out a red flag, and a yellow flag, and a blue flag, and a white flag, and a green flag … on and on and on, until there were flags stretching from one end of the ward to the other.

"Ladies and gentlemen, boys and girls, it is time for the grand finale," cried Mr Wizzy, wondering what the rabbit could possibly find to do for this. Usually, Mr Wizzy took the opportunity to say a quick spell and make himself vanish in a puff of green smoke. Then there would be a drum roll, and he would reappear at the other end of the room.

As Mr Wizzy finished his announcement, the rabbit waved his paw and the whole ward disappeared. Mr Wizzy, the children, the doctors, the nurses and the rabbit found themselves sitting on a grassy bank outside in the warm sunshine. This was all the more extraordinary as it had been a grey, cold day outside only five minutes before.

The illusion lasted only for a minute. Then everyone was back in the ward and the audience was clapping and cheering more loudly than any audience had ever applauded Mr Wizzy before.

"More! More! More!" cried the children, stamping their feet. Their cheeks were pink and their eyes were bright. All of them looked much, much better than they had when Mr Wizzy arrived.

But Mr Wizzy knew better than to push his luck. He packed up his things and waved to the children. Then he hurried home in his little car.

Mr Wizzy dreaded to think what he would see as he approached his house. Sure enough, Mrs Bizzybee's home was surrounded by vans with aerials on top and dozens of eager reporters were hammering at the door. Clearly, the extraordinary things that had happened to Mrs Bizzybee were secret no more. Soon *everyone* would know.

Mr Wizzy crept into his house through the back door. He had no wish to see his face all over that evening's television news programmes. As usual, he put away his equipment and opened the basket with his animal helpers, so that they could hop and fly about freely in the conjuror's sitting room.

"Only," said Mr Wizzy sadly to himself, "I'm not a conjuror any more. If only I hadn't said that stupid spell. Now I don't even have my magic to try to put things right. Whatever am I going to do?"

"I could do it," said the rabbit.

Mr Wizzy rubbed his eyes. He was so miserable that the events at the hospital had become a great blur in his mind. Now he remembered the amazing tricks that the rabbit had done. (And in case you're wondering, the rabbit never had spoken until that day.)

"I could probably put things right," said the rabbit again.

Mr Wizzy made a big effort to concentrate. "I don't understand," he said. "What has happened?"

"Most people don't realise," said the rabbit, "that there is always the same amount of magic in the world. It may pass from one person to another, but it does not grow greater or less. When your magic left you because of the spell on Mrs Bizzybee, I was the nearest creature who could use it properly, so it came to me. After all, I've been watching you do your tricks for *years*. What do you think of my show so far?"

"It was wonderful," said Mr Wizzy. "I particularly liked the falling stars. They were truly magical, I thought. One or two parts could do with a little more polish, perhaps, but we could work on those together. Oh!"

"Yes?" said the rabbit.

"Well, I just realised how things are going to be from now on. I'll be *your* assistant, instead of the other way round."

"That's right," said the rabbit, "and in time, maybe some of the magic will start slipping back from me to you. Who knows?"

Mr Wizzy slumped back in his chair with relief. It was going to be all right. He would still be able to cheer people up and make them smile, he just wouldn't be playing the same part.

"No time to relax now!" cried the rabbit. "We still have to sort out the muddle with Mrs Bizzybee. We can't leave things as they are."

"No, of course not," replied the ex-conjuror. "I have thought about it, but the only idea I had was to wind back time so that none of what happened this afternoon really happened."

"No," said the rabbit, "that won't be possible. That would mean that you never said the silly spell, so you never lost your magic powers. I'm not allowed to do that. But I did have another idea. We could simply do a forgetting spell so that no one remembers that anything strange happened. And maybe a bit of a remembering-wrong spell so that the awkward bits are tidied up."

"But won't that take away *your* magic," asked Mr Wizzy.

"No," said the rabbit. "Mrs Bizzybee is terribly worried at the moment that *she* can't remember what happened. This will sort it all out for her."

So the rabbit said a spell rather quietly, so that Mr Wizzy couldn't hear, and from the window they watched as the television and news reporters drove away, scratching their heads.

The next moment, Mrs Bizzybee rang the front door bell – several times!

Mr Wizzy found himself shaking in his shoes as he went to answer it. As usual, his neighbour began talking as soon as he opened the door.

"Oh-Mr-Wizzy-I-haven't-had-a-minute-to-myself-since-that-incredible-lottery-win-I-felt-I-just-had-to-step-across-and-say-hello-what-do-you-think-of-me-now-that-month-on-a-health-farm-did-me-the-world-of-good-and-I-did-buy-one-or-two-little-bits-and-pieces-for-myself-but-of-course-most-of-the-money-will-be-going-to-the-twins-such-a-surprise-but-everyone-is-delighted-all-my-girls-wanted-children-as-much-as-I-wanted-grandchildren-but-*three*-sets-of-twins-well-it's-amazing-only-they-do-run-in-my-family-you-know-oh-yes-my-Great-Uncle-Barneybee-was-a-twin-and-so-now-I-come-to-think-of-it-was…"

"Mrs Bizzybee, I'm *delighted*," said Mr Wizzy quickly, as Mrs Bizzybee drew breath. "Now I know what a busy grandmother you must be, so I'll come round tomorrow to hear *all* about it."

Exhausted, Mr Wizzy staggered back to the sitting room, where the rabbit was having a nice chat with the dove about the best place to hide during the tricks.

"Everything is all right," said the ex-conjuror. "I don't quite understand what she was talking about when she mentioned twins, but never mind. Now what I need is a nice cup of tea."

Mr Wizzy was just about to get up and go into the kitchen, when he found that he already had a steaming cup of tea in his hand!

The rabbit gave him a wink. "It was to give *you* pleasure," he said, "so I was able to do it."

"You know," smiled Mr Wizzy, "I believe I like this arrangement better than the last one!"

The
Christmas
Pudding
Wish

Once upon a time there was a little boy who wanted more than anything else to have a baby brother. He would mention it casually to his parents as often as he dared.

"What a pity," he would say, as he looked at the seesaw in the park, "that I don't have a little brother to play on *that* with. It would be so much fun."

Or when his parents were taking him shopping, he would look at toys in the shop windows and say, wistfully, "That drum is much too young for *me*, but it would be perfect for a much smaller boy, wouldn't it?"

But although his parents smiled and even sometimes laughed at his comments, he never seemed to be any nearer to having a little baby brother.

Freddie, for that was his name, remembered that Georgia at playgroup had told him about her own little brother being born. "I didn't know what was happening," she said, "but there was a lot of whispering one night and Mum didn't want any supper. Then, in the morning, there he was, tucked up in a cot beside Mum's bed."

After that, Freddie kept a sharp eye on his mother. "Are you sure

you feel hungry?" he would ask
her. "Wouldn't you rather go
without supper tonight? You're
not exactly *thin,* you know."

"Yes, I definitely do want
supper!" laughed his mother,
"and no more comments about
how fat I am, if you don't mind!
I must have a little word with
you about that in any case."

But Freddie had rushed off to
play with his toys. He really
wasn't very interested while his
mother was so definitely eating
her supper.

A few weeks later, Freddie's
mother began to make
preparations for Christmas.

"Isn't it a bit early, Mum?" asked Freddie. "Christmas is a long way away. We haven't even started practising carols at playgroup yet!"

"I may be rather busy nearer Christmas," explained his mother, "which reminds me, Freddie…" But Freddie had gone to watch his favourite video.

Later that week, Mum called Freddie into the kitchen.

"I'm making the Christmas pudding," she said. "The mixture is in this bowl. Now, you must give it a big stir and wish as hard as you can for something you really want. Can you do that?"

Freddie took the bowl and looked at the brown mixture. It smelled sweet and Christmassy. He was just about to put in one tiny finger for a taste, when his mother called out.

"No tasting, Freddie," she said, "or your wish may not come true, you know."

Well, that was too big a risk to take. Freddie knew exactly what he wanted to wish for – and so do you, I expect. He gave a big, big stir and wished for a baby brother to play games with. Then he had another stir and another wish just to be on the safe side.

"I've finished," he told Mum.

A couple of days later, Freddie saw his mother push away her plate of breakfast cereal. But it wasn't supper, so he didn't think anything more about it. It was true that his parents were doing a lot of whispering in the hall, but he didn't think anything about that either, because it was time for playgroup.

Freddie's father made a couple of phone calls in a quiet voice.

"Aunty May will take you to playgroup today," he said. "Mummy and I have to go into town this morning."

Freddie was surprised, but he assumed that Mum and Dad were

going to buy him his Christmas presents, even if Christmas was still a few weeks away.

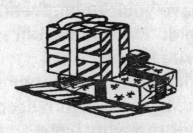

"One of those new racing games would be good," he called helpfully. That made Mum and Dad laugh out loud.

"Oh, I think we can do better than that this year!" said Dad, helping Mum on with her coat.

That morning, Freddie had a lovely time at playgroup. When it

was time to go home, he found
Aunty May waiting for him again.

"You can come home with me
and have your lunch, Freddie,"
she said. "I've got all your
favourite things."

Freddie went off happily with
Aunty May, although it seemed
as if her thoughts were
somewhere else. Every time the
phone rang, she jumped and ran
to answer it. But it was always
just someone wanting to visit
her, or to sell her something to
do with windows.

After an afternoon of playing,
Freddie was feeling quite tired.
He wondered when his Aunty

would take him home to have his supper and go to bed.

"Well, you might just be going to stay with me tonight," said Aunty May, "but I'm not quite sure yet."

Not sure? But grown-ups were always sure. Freddie was just going to ask her more, when the phone rang again.

This time Aunty May talked for only a few minutes. Then she laughed and said, "That's lovely! We'll be there in twenty minutes."

Freddie found himself bundled into his coat and his aunt's car. Within seconds, they were driving along the road into town.

Aunty May stopped at a very big building. Inside, there were lots of corridors – like playschool only bigger. Freddie trotted along, holding his aunt's hand. Then, in the distance, he heard a sound that made his little heart jump for joy. It was a baby crying.

A few minutes later, Freddie was hugging his mother and his proud father and looking down at the dearest little baby brother he could have imagined.

"What's his name?" he asked.

Mum and Dad smiled and said something very strange.

"We've decided," they said, "to call him Louise."

The Magic
Trumpet

Doo, doo, de, doo! Doo, doo, de, doo! Whatever was that noise? Major Bellamy woke and sat up so quickly that he bumped his head on the bedside light.

Doo, doo, de, doo! Doo, doo, de, doo! Well, bless my soul, he thought, it sounds like a trumpet.

Major Bellamy was well used to the sound of the trumpet, having spent many years in the army overseas, but he had not heard one since his retirement. He rubbed his eyes and his ears. Had he been dreaming?

Doo, doo, de, doo! Doo, doo, de, doo! There it was again! He most definitely was *not* dreaming.

Major Bellamy pulled on his silk dressing gown with the gold tassels. He would see about this. Someone had clearly broken into his house and was making an unearthly din downstairs. But what idiot would advertise the fact that he was there? To be on the safe side, Major Bellamy picked up the sword that he used to wear with his smartest uniform. He was prepared to do battle, if he must, to defend his property and his home.

Down the stairs crept Major Bellamy. Everything seemed silent down below. Hardly daring to breathe, he pushed open the door of the dining room with his foot. A shaft of moonlight from the window lit the room almost as clearly as day.

There was no one there. Major Bellamy was a brave man. He peered under the table and behind the door. Then he looked thoughtfully at the regimental trumpet hanging on the wall. It couldn't have played by itself. Could it?

Major Bellamy shook his head.
"Too much cheese for supper,"
he muttered. But just then …
doo, doo, de, doo! And louder
still … DOO, DOO, DE, DOO!

Major Bellamy turned back.
This time there was no doubt
about it. The trumpet had played
by itself. He could see that it was
still trembling slightly on the
wall from the effort.

Major Bellamy hesitated for a
minute, but he was no coward.
With one swift movement, he took
the trumpet from the wall. It was
slightly warm, but otherwise it
felt just as it did when he took it
down once a month for polishing.

Thoughtfully, Major Bellamy carried the trumpet through into the sitting room. In fact, he was concentrating so hard on the trumpet that it took him a minute to take in the scene of devastation in front of him.

The whole room looked as if a whirlwind had hit it. Books had been pulled from the shelves. The cushions had been thrown from the chairs and sofa. Pictures were hanging askew on the walls where someone had peeped behind them.

Major Bellamy felt weak at the knees, but he took a deep breath and picked up the telephone.

"Police," he said firmly. "Police, right away, please."

The old soldier replaced the telephone and sat down. He knew that he must not touch anything before the police arrived. Yet he was determined to try to work out, if he could, what had happened.

Obviously, there had been intruders. Just as clearly, the notes of the trumpet had scared them away. But what had they been looking for? And why, after hanging silently on the Major's dining room wall for nearly twenty years, had the trumpet chosen tonight to play?

Major Bellamy looked at the pictures askew on the walls. The thieves had been looking for something very small, if they thought it could be hidden on the back of a picture or, now, wait a minute, this was more like it, they had been looking for a *safe*! And if that was the case, then they were also looking for something that was so valuable they believed it would be kept in a safe.

It took Major Bellamy only a moment to work out what it could be. He had very few valuables, and he didn't for a moment think that someone would break into his house to steal a couple of medals and a pair of silver serving spoons. No, there was only one thing that was worth anything in his home, and that was the Kashmir Ruby.

Major Bellamy remembered now the darkened room in which a dying man had passed the ruby to him.

"I'm giving it to you," he had gasped, between sips of water, "because it must be owned by someone who does not care at all for its value as a jewel. If it falls into the hands of someone who wants it only for the money it is worth, it will bring him or her the worst possible bad luck for ever."

Major Bellamy had taken the jewel from the dying man, and also, yes, that was right, his trumpet – the very same one that the Major now held.

"I know now that you were not trying to protect me," said Major Bellamy to the trumpet, "but those foolish fellows who thought the jewel could bring them happiness. You have saved them from a horrible fate."

The Major left the sitting room and closed the door, pushing the doorstop away with his foot. It glowed red in the moonlight.

Aunt
Bella's
Umbrella

Chloe was not pleased. "Does she *have* to come?" she asked her mother, for the umpteenth time. "*Why* does she have to come?"

"She has to come because she doesn't have enough money to go on holiday, so we've invited her to stay with us for a few days. I've explained that to you, Chloe," replied her mother.

"But she wears funny clothes and she doesn't like television and she *smells* funny," said Chloe.

"Don't be ridiculous," said her mother sharply. "Aunt Bella's clothes are her own business, and she smells of lavender. It's a

lovely perfume. I can't think why you're getting in such a state about this."

Chloe didn't say anything. She knew that her mother wouldn't have any sympathy if she did tell her the real reason. Aunt Bella was going to have to sleep in *her* room, in the bed her sister slept in when she wasn't away on a school trip. When the two girls were together, they had a lovely time, giggling and whispering after the lights were out. Even when Hannah wasn't there, Chloe could have fun creeping out of bed and playing quietly with some of her toys. But Aunt

Bella was a different matter entirely. Chloe was pretty sure *she* wouldn't want to play games. And what if ... what a horrible thought! What if she snored?

Aunt Bella arrived by train that afternoon. Chloe's Dad went to collect her from the station. When they reached home, Aunt Bella had only a battered old suitcase and a bright red umbrella with her. She insisted on putting both of these in Chloe's room, although Chloe's Mum tried hard to get her to leave her umbrella in the hall.

"Oh, no," said Aunt Bella. "This old umbrella comes with me."

That night, Aunt Bella decided to go to bed at the same time as Chloe, which was quite early.

"I'm tired from the journey," she said, "and this way, I won't wake you up when I come in, will I, sweetheart?"

Chloe had hoped to be fast asleep when Aunt Bella went to bed, so that she didn't know anything about it, but she smiled politely and showed her aunt where her towels were and how the bedside light worked.

When Aunt Bella emerged from the bathroom, she was wearing an extraordinary purple dressing gown and curlers in her hair.

Chloe had to stuff her sheets in her mouth to stop herself laughing out loud.

Chloe's mother put her head round the door and smiled as she said, "Goodnight, girls!"

Chloe lay awake in the darkness, listening hard. Could she hear just the tiniest little bit of snoring?

"No, she doesn't snore," said a voice from the other side of the room in a friendly way.

"Oh! I didn't say it out loud, did I?" asked Chloe, before she had time to think.

"No, of course not," replied her aunt, in quite a different kind of voice, "but sometimes he can tell what you're thinking."

"Who can?" asked Chloe.

"My umbrella, of course. He's magic and helps me to do all kinds of things."

Chloe thought for a moment.

"It's true," said the umbrella. "She's not completely batty."

"Oh, I'm sorry," gasped Chloe. "I didn't mean to think that. It just popped into my head."

"Don't worry," said Aunt Bella. "But you just behave yourself, umbrella! Just be a little bit more careful about what you say."

"All right," said the umbrella, "but I should just mention that this little girl thinks that your dressing gown is pretty funny as well, you know."

"Well, she's entitled to her opinion," said Aunt Bella. "Now, where shall we go tonight, umbrella?"

"I was wondering about a trip to Venice," said the umbrella carelessly. "I've heard it's not too crowded at this time of year."

"Lovely," said Aunt Bella. "Now, Chloe, shut your eyes and think about umbrellas."

Chloe couldn't believe this was happening, but she did as she was told. She imagined umbrellas in all kinds of colours. They began to whirl about before her eyes, faster and faster.

"Now open your eyes," said Aunt Bella. Chloe found herself in a little boat, gliding along a canal between tall buildings. In front of her was her aunt, holding her umbrella over her head like a parasol.

"This is Venice," said Aunt Bella. "It's beautiful, isn't it?"

"But where is it?" asked Chloe. "It doesn't look like anywhere I know at all."

"It's in a country called Italy," explained Aunt Bella, "a long, long way from your home. Do you like it?"

"I'd like one of those ice creams over there," replied Chloe. She had just spotted a man with a little stall on one side of the canal.

Five minutes later, Chloe had her mouth full of the tastiest ice cream she had ever eaten. But Aunt Bella's umbrella began to flutter above her head.

"Oops a daisy," said Aunt Bella. "It looks as though it's time to go home. Shut your eyes, Chloe."

The next minute, Chloe found herself back in her own little bed.

"Time to sleep, now," said Aunt Bella. "We can go travelling again tomorrow night, if you like."

Chloe could hardly count the wonderful places she visited over the next few nights, but all too soon it was time for Aunt Bella to go home.

"You were a good girl to share your room," said Chloe's mother, as they waved Aunt Bella off in the train. "She has so few chances to get away, I felt we had to help."

"I'm not so sure about that," said Chloe quietly, "but I'm very glad you invited her *here*. And her umbrella."

Chloe's mother wasn't sure she had heard her daughter properly. She couldn't mind about an umbrella, could she?

The
Contrary
Princess

Once upon a time there was a Princess who was very cross and difficult. She disagreed with everything that was said to her, just for the sake of it. And because she was a Princess, everyone agreed with her, however silly she was being.

You wouldn't believe how annoying the Princess could be. Suppose someone came to visit her and said, "That is a beautiful dress you are wearing, Your Highness." The Princess would immediately reply, "This is an awful, ugly dress. I can't bear the sight of it. I shall take it off at once." If someone praised a clump of flowers in the royal garden, she would at once declare that they were common and uninteresting, and she would order the gardeners to dig them up at once.

This ridiculous state of affairs went on for some time, until one day a fairy happened to be passing when the Princess was being particularly contrary. (As a matter of fact, it wouldn't have made very much difference when the fairy had flown by, as the Princess was always the same.)

As the fairy flew past, she heard the Princess declare, "It doesn't matter what you say,

Father, you are sure to be wrong, and I shall be right." Now, apart from the fact that this was not at all a nice way to speak to the King, it was also a really very silly thing to say. No one is right all the time. And no one is wrong all the time for that matter.

"Very well," said the fairy, "if you must be so contrary, I will make sure that everything you say is exactly the opposite of what you mean – always." She said a quick spell, and the deed was done.

That evening, a maid servant brought the Princess her supper. "The cook has asked me to tell you that the soup is particularly delicious today," she said.

The Princess tasted a spoonful. "Yes," she said, "this is the most delicious soup I have ever tasted."

The maid servant almost dropped her tray in amazement. Had she heard correctly? Had the Princess actually liked something?

The Princess was just as amazed. That hadn't been what she had meant to say at all – far from it. But the maid was smiling and making an extra low curtsey, instead of flouncing off as she often did.

Next morning, the King came to his daughter and suggested that they go riding together.

"That would be delightful," said the Princess, much to her own amazement. The King was so touched that he had tears in his eyes. It was a very, very long time since his daughter had shown any kindness towards a member of her own family.

In fact, the King and the Princess spent a very pleasant morning. The Princess agreed that the countryside was beautiful and her father's horse was spirited. She confessed that the castle looked very handsome

on its hill and that, yes, perhaps it was time she considered finding a Prince and setting up a home of her own.

The King was amazed and delighted. His daughter seemed to be growing up at last, and he could not have been more pleased that she was seriously considering settling down.

The Princess, on the other hand, was confused and a little frightened. Not one of the nice things she had said had been in her mind before they popped out of her mouth. And as for getting married, nothing was further from her thoughts! But all the same, it was rather touching to see her father looking so happy.

The King lost no time in setting about finding a husband for his precious daughter. All the Princes from nearby lands were invited to a grand ball at the palace.

On the evening of the ball, the Princess wore her most magnificent dress. She looked down from the balcony at all the young men who had gathered to pay court to her and found that she despised them all. Yet, when one of them asked whether she would like to dance, she found herself telling him that nothing could be more charming.

Altogether, the more horrible the Princess wanted to be, the more friendly and pleasant she found herself seeming. It was intensely annoying.

Now one Prince had been watching the Princess very closely. When she withdrew to a nearby room for a moment to catch her breath, he slipped in behind her.

"Your Highness," he said, gently. "Can you really be charmed by so many different Princes? Are you not deceiving us all?"

The Princess looked at him gratefully, as if to say, "Yes, you are right, so right!" but out of her mouth came the words, "No, Sir, I find you all equally delightful."

Then the Prince told the Princess what he really thought. "I believe that you have been bewitched, Your Highness," he said. "If you will allow me, I can lift the spell and return you to yourself."

"Please don't," said the Princess, but her eyes said otherwise.

The Prince stepped forward and kissed the Princess, which at once broke the fairy's spell.

"Forgive me," said the Prince. "It was the only way to undo the magic. Now you may be as horrid to me as you like."

But after a month of having her nasty comments changed to nice ones, the Princess suddenly found that what she wanted to say more than anything else was the truth.

"Sir," she said, "You told me that I was bewitched before, but now I believe you have bewitched me again." And she kissed the Prince, to show him exactly what she meant.

The Prince and the Princess have been married for a year now. The Princess always says exactly what she means, and so does the Prince. You have only to look at them to see that this suits them very well indeed.

Wise
Wishes

Every day, we make wishes. "I wish the sun would shine," we say, when we want to have a picnic. "I wish it would rain," we say, when we want to avoid going for a long walk with an energetic uncle.

If you think about it, you will realise that everyone simply

cannot have all their wishes
come true all the time. After all,
your energetic uncle is probably
wishing for sunshine, just as you
are wishing for rain.

Now wishes are magical things,
and magic needs to be taken
very seriously indeed. It can do
wonderful things, and it can do
terrible things. You need to be
very careful what you wish for.

Once upon a time, there was a
little boy. When he watched his
elder brothers playing together,
he wanted so much to join in.
But his brothers laughed. "You're
much too young to play with us,"
they said.

So the little boy shut his eyes and wished with all his heart. "I wish I could be older," he said, and pretty soon, he was.

A few years later, the boy's brothers began to get married. The boy met a lovely girl who was as pretty as she was clever. "Will you be my wife?" he asked.

But the pretty girl just laughed. "You're much too young to be married," she said.

Once again, the boy shut his eyes and made his wish. "I wish I could be older," he said, and very soon, he was.

The boy married the pretty girl and settled down. He wanted to earn lots of money for his wife and growing family, so he went to his employer and asked to be made a partner in the company.

"My boy," laughed his boss, "you're much too young to be made a partner."

The boy – who was a man now – closed his eyes and wished from the bottom of his heart. "I wish I could be older," he said, and in the twinkling of an eye, he was.

The man became a partner in his company and did well. His children grew up and left home.

Then the man began to be tired of working every day. He went to the other partners and said, "I have been thinking about the path my life has taken, and I should like to retire very soon."

But the other partners laughed. "You're much too young to retire," they said. "We need you here."

Then the man shut his eyes and wished with all his power. "I wish I could be older," he said, and in no time at all, he was.

So the man retired from his business and enjoyed playing with his grandchildren. But the day came when they ran away from him, laughing, and called, "You can't catch us, Grandpa. You're much too old!"

It was true. Then the man sat down, for he was feeling tired, and he wished harder than he had ever wished in his life. "I wish," he said, "I could be younger."

It is a strange thing that all the other wishes he had ever made came true. But his last wish never did.

If I could wish one thing for you, dear reader, it is that you should take more care with your own wishes than that poor man.

Are there many kinds of wishes?
No, there are only two:
Those that bring us what we wish
And those that never do.

The
Apple Spell

Once there was a little girl who loved apples more than anything else in the world. She would have eaten apples for breakfast, lunch and supper if her mother had let her.

She was rather a greedy little girl, too. She couldn't help feeling that every apple someone else ate was an apple she couldn't eat herself! When you think of all the apples there are in the world, that was really very silly, wasn't it?

One day when she was out walking, the little girl, whose name was Bessie, saw an old lady, sitting by the side of the road. Next to her was a basket of beautiful apples.

"Hello, sweetheart," said the old lady in a quavering voice, "can you help me, please?"

Bessie slowly went over to the old lady. She felt annoyed that her walk had been interrupted.

"I sat down here for a moment for a rest," explained the old lady, "and I can't persuade my poor old legs to get up again.

I just need a bit of a heave-ho from a big, strong girl like you."

Bessie's eyes grew brighter as she saw the big basket of apples, and she had an idea.

"I'll help you," she said, "if you will give me one of your apples."

Now the old lady would have offered the little girl an apple for her kindness, but being asked for something is rather different.

"And if I don't give you an apple?" asked the old lady, looking sharply at Bessie. "I just want to be sure I understand."

Bessie blinked. She hadn't really thought that far. She wasn't really an unpleasant girl, but now that she thought about it, a bargain was a bargain.

"Well, if you don't" she said, "I suppose I shall leave you here."

"I see," said the old lady. "Very well, my dear. I will give you an apple when you have helped me to my feet." And she stretched out her gnarled old hands.

Bessie seized the old woman and gave a big pull.

"Heave-ho!" chuckled the old lady, and she hopped so nimbly to her feet that Bessie was surprised she had needed help.

"Well, thank you very much, my dear," said the old lady cheerfully. "Goodbye!"

She picked up her basket and set off down the road.

"Just a minute," cried Bessie loudly. "What about my apple?"

The old lady paused. "I was just giving you one last chance," she said under her breath, holding out the basket.

Bessie picked the rosiest, roundest apple she could see. It looked so delicious that she immediately took a huge bite.

"Goodbye again!" called the old lady.

"Ooooeye!" cried Bessie.

"You shouldn't talk with your mouth full, dear," said the old lady, smiling.

"I aah ehh iii oww o iii oww!" said Bessie.

The old lady knew perfectly well what she was trying to say. When Bessie took a huge bite of the apple, it had become stuck in her mouth. She could neither munch through it nor pull her teeth out of it. It was really a most *un*glamorous situation to be in!

"I should have thought, my dear," said the old lady, "that you would be happy to be *always* eating something you are so very fond of." And she turned away.

You may have guessed by now that the old lady had magic

powers. A tiny spell was making
Bessie very, very uncomfortable.

What if she could never speak
again? What if she could never
eat anything else ever again?
Bessie's eyes filled with tears.

The old lady looked thoughtful
for a moment. She could see that
the little girl really was feeling
sorry for herself – and perhaps

she was feeling a little bit sorry about her behaviour too. She said a few words under her breath, and Bessie's apple fell to the ground.

"I'm sorry," sobbed Bessie. "I know I was greedy."

The old lady smiled gently. "Sometimes unpleasant things can teach us a great deal about ourselves," she said. "Now this time, I really will say goodbye, my dear."

When Bessie looked up, the old lady had vanished!

Bessie hurried home, where her mother was preparing supper for the family.

"I'm glad you're here, Bessie," she said. "Supper is nearly ready. I've made your favourite dessert, too. Apple pie!"

Bessie felt a little faint. Somehow she felt that she couldn't face another apple.

You know, that little girl has been a much nicer person recently. She helps at home and tries very hard to think about other people and not about what *she* wants all the time.

Oh, and what is her favourite food in all the world? Why, bananas, of course!

The Elf
Who
Couldn't
Spell

Once upon a time, there was a little elf who would *not* pay attention at school. He would look out of the window, or draw pictures in his book, or simply float away in a world of his own, imagining what it would be like to be a grown-up elf.

As you know, it is always very important to listen carefully during lessons. At any moment, you may learn something that will be useful to you five minutes later or for the rest of your life.

It is a great pity that Elderberry Elf was not paying attention one Tuesday morning last autumn when Mrs Maple was teaching one of her interesting classes in Elementary Magic.

"Now remember," she said, "these words must *always* be used at the end of each spell. If they are not, then you will not be able to undo the spell. Are you listening, Elderberry?"

"Yes, Mrs Maple," said the little elf. "We must always use those words at the end of a spell, so that we can undo it if we want to."

"Good," said Mrs Maple. "If there is one thing you must remember from everything I teach you this year, it is that."

Well, it *sounded* as though Elderberry understood, and in a way he did, but there was one big problem. *He couldn't remember what "those words" were!* Elderberry knew that he *should* ask his teacher, but he couldn't quite bring himself to admit he had not been listening. And the longer he left it, the harder it became to ask the question. From time to time, the little elf worried about those words he did not know, but usually he tried not to think about it.

Now, I'm sure you're imagining that something dreadful happened to Elderberry. Did he turn himself into a cabbage and have to stay like that? Did he take a magic trip to Peru, and is he still there? Well, no. What Elderberry did was to try out a little magic to make him forget all the spells he had learnt. This is a useful spell to use on evil wizards, of course, but it is better to practise on yourself first … if you remember "those words" so that you can reverse it.

The result is that Elderberry now cannot do any magic at all. This sometimes makes him sad, but I think that we are all much, much safer that way. If you see Elderberry, you won't tell him any of *your* magic, will you?

Titles in this Series *include*

The Curious Kitten
The Enchanted Treasure
The Sleepy Teddy Bear
The Clever Little Rabbit
The First Little Fairy
The Elegant Elf
The Friendly Pig
The Busy Baker
The Smiling Star
The Forgetful Squirrel